Marx Joyce
Defoe Abbott Hardy Machiavelli Chesterton Cooper Emerson Austen
Melville Montaigne Haggard Hugo Grimm
Stoker Carroll Christie Byron Eliot
Wilde Maupassant Molière
Garnett Einstein Fitzgerald Engels Schiller
Goethe Hawthorne Smith Kafka
Cotton Dostoyevsky Hall
Baum Henry Kipling Doyle Willis
Leslie Dumas Flaubert Turgenev Nietzsche
Stockton Vatsyayana Balzac
Curtis Tocqueville Verne Crane
Homer Widger Tolstoy Gogol Vinci
Darwin Whitman Busch
Potter Freud Thoreau Twain Scott
Kant Zola Lawrence Plato Harte
Jowett Stevenson Dickens Burton Hesse
Andersen Cervantes
London Descartes Voltaire
Poe Aristotle Wells
Hale James Hastings Cooke
Bunner Shakespeare Irving
Richter Chambers
Doré Dante Chekhov Benedict Alcott
Swift da Shaw Wodehouse Pushkin
Newton

The Treason and Death of Benedict Arnold A Play for a Greek Theatre

John Jay Chapman

Imprint

This book is part of TREDITION CLASSICS

Author: John Jay Chapman
Cover design: Buchgut, Berlin – Germany

Publisher: tredition GmbH, Hamburg - Germany
ISBN: 978-3-8472-1234-8

www.tredition.com
www.tredition.de

THE TREASON & DEATH

OF

BENEDICT ARNOLD

A PLAY FOR A GREEK THEATRE

BY

JOHN JAY CHAPMAN

MOFFAT, YARD & COMPANY
1910

CHARACTERS

BENEDICT ARNOLD.

JOSHUA SMITH.

MAJOR ANDRÉ.

MRS. ARNOLD.
  WILLIAM ARNOLD, *A Boy of Eight, Son to Benedict.*

FATHER HUDSON.
  CHORUS OF WAVES (*Men*).
  CHORUS OF CLOUDS (*Women*).

CHORUS-LEADER OF MEN.

CHORUS-LEADER OF WOMEN.

TREASON.

DEATH.

TWO PICKETS.

A SERVANT.

SCENE

ACT I. THE SHORE OF THE HUDSON NEAR WEST POINT.

ACT II. SITTING-ROOM OF BENEDICT ARNOLD IN ENGLAND IN 1801.

The Acts are Separated by a Short Vocal Intermezzo.

TREASON AND DEATH

OF BENEDICT ARNOLD

ACT I

The margin of the Hudson at West Point. Fort Putnam and the Highlands in the distance. A flag is fluttering on the fort. The orchestra represents the level of the river shore, upon which level the Chorus will enter. The characters of the drama appear on a bank or platform, slightly raised above the orchestra and Chorus. At the opening of the play Father Hudson is upon the scene. He reclines in the centre of the stage in the attitude of a river-god. The nook or couch in which he rests is situated between the two levels, as it were in an angle of the river bank. His position is such that he can, by turning his head, either watch the personages on the stage, or address the Chorus on the river margin. He is so painted and disposed as not to attract attention when the play opens, but to appear rather as a part of the scenery and decoration.

First Picket. Uneasy has been my watch. Dark have been my forebodings, standing first on one foot and then on the other, through the night hours, preyed upon by visions, holding my eyelids open by my will, while strange thoughts like vultures over their carrion, wheeling about above me, assail me, tear me with their beaks and talons. Dark looms the cloud bank through the black portals of the river. The fog holds the bleared eyes of the morning. And I, stiff with watching, suspect some evil. Some foul play is in the mountains, stalking in the shadows of the dawn. Would God the releasing trumpet would blow and the flag flutter on the mountain side, and that I might find all well! General Washington is on a journey. Would God he were returned! [*The sound of a bugle is heard.*] Blow, blessed bugle! Blow to the rising Sun! Blow to the dayspring of Liberty, to the new nation rising calmly above the dangers that beset her dawn. Blow bugle, and scatter the night-thoughts of terror!

[*Enter the relieving* Picket.] Who goes there?

Second Picket. A friend and thy relief.
  Our post is changed;
  The pickets are extended up the hills,
  And this low post abandoned.

First Picket. That is strange,
  To leave the river front without a watch!
  If we expect attack, attack must come
  Along the river, — —

Second Picket. Comrade, spare your brains,
  And take your orders. [*Exeunt* Pickets.]

Father Hudson. Daughters of the sky, ye clouds of the morning,
  Replenishers of my veins, ye purple, wandering clouds!
  And you, ye waves that lap my feet, far-traveling,
    restless, endlessly moving!
  Thralls of the circling ocean, waves of the sea —
  Attend your Father Hudson, the Ageless, the Majestic!
  Calling to you, his sons and daughters, summoning you at his
need.
  Stoop, daughters of ether, ye clouds of the mountains!
  Rise, sons of the sea, most ancient retainers,
  Flow towards your father's need! the River calls —
  Father Hudson summons his children.

[*Enter simultaneously* Chorus of Waves, (*men*) *on one side, and on the
other,* Chorus of Clouds (*women*). *They flock slowly into the orchestra,
approaching each other, and sing as they assemble.*]

Both Choruses. Father Hudson, we are coming, we are streaming,
    we are foaming
  From the sky and from the earth,
    Down the mountains,
    Through the fountains,
  We are streaming, steaming forth;
    We, the children of your will,

12

Born to serve you, and to fill
All your banks and all your margin
  With the fulness of enlarging,
  With the plentitude of rivers,
  We, the generous water-givers,
Overflowing, bubbling, swelling,
Feed you with our rich upwelling.

Chorus of Men. From Monadnock and Mount Washington—
  And where the haughty deer on Hudson's Bay
  Sniffs the north wind, We bring you Mist.

Chorus of Women. From the rank lowlands of the Delaware,
  And from the even margin of low sand,
  Where the Atlantic smites the continent, We bring you Salt.

Chorus of Men. From Sicily and the Cumacan Cave,
  And from the mountains where Apollo's shafts
  Whitened the hillsides once, We bring you Thought.

Chorus of Women. From the dark heart of man that scorns the light,
  From Wisdom, found in Meekness through Despair, We bring you
Grief.

Both Choruses. Haste to where our father dwells!
  We the movers, we the rovers,
  Come to your eternal dwelling.
  Ancient father, we will bring
  News and thought of everything,
  From the mossy citadels,
  And the cities of the sea;
  Timeworn tales of prophecy
  We are bringing in our singing
  To your newer Majesty.
  To your destiny belated,
  Young and unsophisticated,
  We, the children of the ages,
  Bring the solemn heritages,—
  Force and Woe and Human Fate,—

Embittering your god-like state.
Bitter is life!
Bitter, bitter even to the gods, is life!

Father Hudson. Sons and daughters, sole feeders of my life,
  By these new-coming white men I am destroyed.
  My feet are burned in Manhattan, my thighs in the Mohawk,
  While in the Adirondacks they blaze enduring ruin.

[*The leaders speak, not sing, except as otherwise noted.*]

Leader of Men. Alas! little knows he that his kingdom is of nothing but of change and pain.

Leader of Women. Foolish god that must await the baptism of humanity!

Leader of Men. Father! these things must be: therefore endure. Lo, thy old trees are as grass; thy ancient summits as fresh ant-hills. Chaldea sends thee this message, father; Egypt salutes thee; Greece sends thee this song; a song of tribulation. For there is no short cut to Antiquity: therefore endure.

Father Hudson. Woe, woe, woe is me!

Leader of Men. Untutored God! Mind ragged as thy hills, thou must accept the refining pain.

Father Hudson. Woe, woe, woe is me!

Leader of Women. Peace, Father! Do not whine. Because thou hast been spared thou art soft-minded. Because thou wast spared thou art a child.

Leader of Men. When thy hills shall have been steeped for a thousand years in history, then thou wilt be patient.

Leader of Women. What thou feelest is not the axe nor the firebrand, but the Spirit of Man moving in thy demesnes.

Leader of Men. Lo, where it comes! Lo, where the shadow falls!

[*Enter* Benedict Arnold. *He is in the Uniform of an American General. He limps.*]

Both Choruses. A light thing is man and his suffering very little.

If he can but endure for a short time, death saves him. Lo, his release cometh and his happiness is long.

Fame forever follows in the steps of the just man: an unending life springs up behind him.

Children follow him: a good father's life is a lamp that burns in the heart of the son.

How short is the struggle of the greatest hero, and how long his fame!
Save me from pride and from the expectation of praise from men.

Arnold. He may not come. —
   What if it were a ruse to capture me? —
   The whole proceeding cloaked in infamy,
   And no faith in the matter?
   André should be here. André is a man
   Of sterling honor, and will keep his faith.
   My secret's in his hand. — My change of heart
   Must to His Majesty have long been known,
   And he will praise me for it. Civil war
   Knows no such thing as treason; change of sides,
   The victory of reason in the heart,
   Makes Loyalist turn Whig. Montgomery,
   Richard Montgomery, was honor's darling;
   And when his body fell, scaling Quebec,
   Down the sheer rock it left a track of light
   Which sped in opposition towards the stars
   Bearing his fame. He was an officer
   In the King's army ere he found our own.
   Did conscience fret the gallant Irishman
   To think what uniform was on his back
   When he so died? What if in that assault
   I had died too, my name had ranked with his
   In song and monument; unfading laurels
   Had shed their brazen lustre o'er our brows,
   And we, like demigods, had lived forever.
   Was it enough for *him*, to scale the sky

Against the slippery adamant of Fame,
And, giving youth, give all? I have done more.
All of his early prowess was mine too:
In everything I match him; and to me
Remains the hell of glory on the Lakes,
When with my hand I stopped the British fleet,—
Stayed them a year: they dreaded to come on.
And I had done it. There remain my fights
At Ridgefield, and those shortened days
At Saratoga, when the fit came on
And I knew nothing but the act of war,
And victory coming down, Victory, Victory!
'Twas I that saved them! Yes, 'twas I that saved you—
Ye little wranglers with the name of war!
I beat Burgoyne, I saved the continent,
The Continental Army and the Cause,
Washington, Congress, and the whole of you,
I saved ye,—saved ye,—and I had for it—
It chokes me still to say it—had for it—
It wakes me in the night with leaping hatred,—
Out of my bed I leap to think of it,—
Hitting me in my sleep the poison comes
And fangs my heart.—I had a *Reprimand*!
I, reprimanded by a sorry crew
Of politicians—I, I, I——!
Thus, in my heart for sixteen months of hurt,
Burns the injustice, clamors the revenge.
No, no revenge! but justice,
Nothing but justice—I'll have justice!

Both Choruses. Foolish is the man who thinks upon his wrongs though they be great. The sting is in him; the poison is in himself.

Lo, he accuses others, and the deed of his death is done with his own hand.

Father Hudson. What is the man disturbed about, my children?

Leader of Men. He is a hero and a battle-god:
  The spoils and the rewards he justly won,

Others have seized, and left his haughty heart
A withered laurel.

Father Hudson. Surely it was wrong;
  The hero should receive the hero's meed.

Leader of Men. The gods that made him hero had left out
  The drop of meekness which preserves the rest
  From self-destruction.

  Father Hudson. Will he kill himself?

Leader of Men. More than a suicide. —
  A living death
  Takes up its habitation in his heart.

Father Hudson. Little I understand, but greatly pity.
  You, who have mastered all philosophy,
  Can surely soothe him.

Leader of Men. None can reach the man.
  He is beyond the boundaries of speech,
  And goes the paths of blindness.
  Would'st thou, O Father, see the invisible,
  And know what agitates your placid mind?

  Father Hudson. Show me: I can receive it.

  [*The following Invocation is sung by the* Leader of the Women *in a clear contralto voice.*]

Leader of Women. Spirit of the unseen habitation,
  Walking distress,
  Blighting presence, Nemesis, Evil,
  Good-in-Darkness,
  Passing from breast to breast,
  Reaching easily all men,
  And the vine in the orchard,
  And the thick clusters of the grape,
  And the bending branches of the young peach trees,

When the south wind blows death upon their pride, —
O intimate undoing! In what form walkest thou here?

Treason. [*Without.*] Who calls?

Leader of Men. One who knows thee well enough: thou need'st not hide.

[*Enter* Treason.]

Leader of Men. [*To* Father Hudson.] Behold the unsleeping fiend that lives in him! His name is Treason.

Treason. Art thou there, Benedict?

Arnold. [*Aside.*] Why not? 'Tis Fame,
  Reward, wealth, power, revenge and simple justice
  All at a clap. They'll make a Lord of me, —
  Pacificator of the Colonies, —
  Restorer of an erring people's love
  To their forgiving Sovereign. At a clap!
  The key to all of this is in my hand, —
  West Point; and in my other hand,
  Sir Henry's promises, — money in sums,
  To weigh the unweighed treasures I have sunk
  For these damned ingrates.

Treason. Art thou there, Benedict?

Arnold. [*Still aside.*] They took my all,
  Engulfed my freely-given wealth, paid out
  For their salvation; now they count the cost,
  File my accounts and give me promises, —
  Hopes for next year. Twas not in coin like that
  I paid at Saratoga!

Treason. Benedict!

Arnold. Who art thou, spirit of the inner world? I cannot see thee.

Treason. And yet you called me.

Arnold. No, I called thee not. I called to mind
  My bullet-shattered thigh, and the hot thirst
  Of fever. Did not Washington himself
  Send me the sword-knots he received from France,
  And Congress vote a horse caparisoned
  To bear me proudly?

Treason. Ay; they kept back that
  Which all out-weighed the rest.

Arnold. My rank!
  My rank!
  Five brigadiers promoted over me!

  Treason. They paid with compliment.

Arnold. A soldier's rank
  Is, as his guiding genius in the sky,
  A holy thing. That rank which I had earned
  They gave to striplings.

  Treason. Pay them well for it!

  Arnold. Leave me: I do desire to be alone.

Treason. Without me, Arnold, thou art not alone.
  I am beside thee till thy dying breath:
  When Treason leaves, he hands thee unto Death.

Arnold. It is not treason to preserve one's life
  Among wild beasts; nor treason to demand
  The reasonable payment of a debt;
  Nor treason for the savior of a land —
  Listen: — There was a stripling in the town
  Where I was born; and this rash vigorous boy
  Seized by the nose a bull, that in a fright
  Had rushed aboard a crowded ferry-boat,
  And held him through his plunges till he fell,
  Subdued by pain. The boy for no reward,
  But for the devil in him, did the thing.

But had he been a man, and sought reward,
Had he been banged about this rocking world
As I have, holding terror by the horns,
Could he not ask a pittance?—Leave me, friend.
I am exhausted, taking all the brunt
And getting kicks for pay. Nay, leave me, Sir,
The argument is over. Let me rest.

[Sits down and tries to sleep.]

Treason. I'll watch beside thee.

Father Hudson. Can ye not calm him somewhat in his sleep?

Leader of Men. [*To* Treason.] Will you not leave the man and let him rest?

Treason. His sleep is mine. When waking let him rest.

Father Hudson. [*To* Treason.] This is a cruel fate ye mete him out.

Treason. Be it your province to be merciful.

Father Hudson. When will ye leave the man, thou empty ghost?

Treason. When Treason in the flesh shall come to meet him.

Both Choruses. Surely it is a good thing for a hero to die in his youth; for then is he perfect. The bark is not broken on the wand nor the neck worn by the yoke.

Surely young men are better than old; and we praise them deservedly. This man, a few years since, could endure reverse; but now he is broken and worn away: his soul bows down; he cannot hold out longer.

It is a good thing when a young hero dies; for so is he safe. His immortality is meted to him. O spare us a trial like this man's who is on the brink of great misfortune.

Arnold. [*Starting up.*] They have betrayed me! Who goes there?

[*Enter* Joshua Smith. *Exit* Treason.]

Joshua Smith. A friend!

Arnold. His name?

Joshua Smith. Joshua Smith. And yours?

Arnold. Arnold, my man. Good God! you startled me. I must have
slept. What news? Will André come?

Joshua Smith. He's just behind me.
  All is as we planned.
  The British sloop-of-war hangs in the tide.
  The *Vulture* brought him, and she waits for him
  Not two miles to the south. I boarded her. With every point
  Raised in your letters André is agreed;
  And back of him, Sir Henry Clinton stands;
  And back of *him,* — ye'll hear it now? — King George!
  Packt, stamped upon, agreed, and understood,
  The bargain's struck. Your hand, my Lord! Sir Benedict!
  Lord Ruler Benedict, The Lord Protector of the Colonies,
  And Duke of, — what you will. Young André follows.
  I chased ahead to find you. Put it high!
  You'll put the figure high? — I'm out of breath —

Arnold. I'll put it high enough to help a friend. —
  No fear of that, my lad. Go rest awhile:
  Stand sentinel upon the shore below.

[*Exit* Smith. *As he goes out he indicates* Arnold *to* André *by a gesture.*
Enter André. *His slender, refined, almost girlish youth is in contrast with*
Arnold's *battle-worn, gigantic figure.*]

Arnold. [*Aside.*] At last my arrows strike!
  [*To* André.] What! Major André!
  This is a crazy meeting, — somewhat strange
  After your jigging nights in Philadelphia, —
  A *Mischianza,* where we play a masque,
  And act a drama fraught with consequence
  More serious than any since the Duke
  Brought back King Charles. Two true-born Englishmen,
  If you'll accept my hand, shall this day place

A jewel in old England's diadem,
Which some rash spirits would shake out of it.

   André. Have you the papers ready?

   Arnold. They are here; The plans of all the out-posts to the dot,
And every man on duty in the Fortress.

   André. The general is in Hartford?

Arnold. And returns
  Not for some days. Our garrison I'll post
  Distributively on the distant hills;
  While from the *Vulture* half a thousand men
  Land in the darkness. Thus without a blow,
  But with the magic of a countersign,
  West Point becomes your own.

André. Is there some house
  Or tavern, where with more deliberate mind
  We may o'erlook the papers, and make note
  Of our exacter meanings?

Arnold. Close at hand,
  The mansion of my agent, Joshua Smith.

André. Good, we'll go there. O Arnold, death is nothing;
  Our lives are forfeit to our country's cause.
  Which of us would not quit the world in peace
  After some act that scaled the walls of time,
  And stood on the rampart?

Arnold. Right, and bravely said! I've given my life
  As many times as I have mounted horse
  To reconnoitre —

   André. But this is different, Arnold.

Arnold. Different, ay different! it saves men's lives:
  Without a drop of blood it ends a war.

André. You are a veteran, and know the feel
  Of imminent death. I could die bravely, too.

Arnold. Of course you could. All fear is bookish talk
  Cooked up by writers out of literature,
  To give the shudder to dyspeptic girls.
  Dying is easy. Come along, my friend!
  A glass of port shall cure us of such fears;
  Moments like this make mirth in after years.

  [*Exeunt* Arnold *and* André.]

Father Hudson. Is there no way to stop them; can ye not Bring pause to these excited rushing men?

Leader of Men. Pause is unknown, as to your moving waters, That take their God-directed, downward course, Deaf to beseechment.

Father Hudson. 'Tis most pitiful.

Both Choruses. No, not to mirth can my voice be tuned, while these two men converse. Often their story comes to me in the night, and causes weeping.

One, the young troubadour, the boy poet, beloved by all, burning for fame; and, in his innocence, he performs the mean work of a spy.

And the other, the old hero, seven times baptized with immortality-in-action, who betrays his country out of foolishness.

To the first, death by hanging: to the second, one and twenty years of dishonored life.

Which of them shall have most of pity? Which of them could we see again with gladness, or greet with a gay demeanor?

The fate of the young man I deem the better; because he is young, and because death took him in his beauty.

Strange it is what souls are woven together by destiny; and out of what substance life is wrought.

All men become something incredible to themselves; for they are unwound like a cocoon, and know not which way the thread doth run.

They dance like motes in the sunbeam for a moment, and then are illumined no more. Legend takes some of them, and they become pictures; and the rest, it would seem, enter again into nothingness.

Grant me to know the desire of mine own heart beforehand; that I may not be deceived. Give me not much, but a true thing, and one that lasts forever.

[*The distant sound of cannonading is heard.*]

Father Hudson. Surely I hear a sound disquieting—

Leader of Men. Wait: you shall know the cause.

[*Enter hurriedly, and meeting,* Arnold *and* André *on one side,* Joshua Smith *on the other.*]

Joshua Smith. General Arnold! Major André!

Arnold. What is it? What has happened?

Joshua Smith. Colonel Livingston's redoubts on the eastern bank. He has fired on the *Vulture.* They are exchanging shots; and the *Vulture* is dropping down stream. She cannot bear the fire.

Major André. We are lost!

Arnold. No, no, no; not lost, not lost. You have only to drop down stream also. Mr. Smith goes with you; and you shall be put aboard the vessel a few miles below. Eh, Smith?

Joshua Smith. Not for the world, General! It is daylight now, and if I should be seen taking this gentleman to the *Vulture,* the Yankees would shoot both of us.

Arnold. Some truth in that. But what can we do?

Joshua Smith. Go the other way, General. You must give a pass to both Major André and me, allowing us to cross the river, and so on to New York. I'll go with the Major till we reach the British lines. It's a plain road to safety.

André. But my uniform —

Arnold. It is a case for a change of coats.

André. But the countrymen are swarming in every highway —

Joshua Smith. They are all my friends. Every rebel is my friend; — and — harkee, — every Tory is my friend — from Peekskill to New York! You'll be as safe as the General himself, — and much more comfortable, — till you reach the British Headquarters.

Arnold. [*To* André.] He's right, André, he's right. It's a safer way than the other when all's said. He knows every lane in the country. [*More firing.*] Here, take the papers. And God bless you! There's no time to lose. This pass covers all routes. The patriots know my hand and respect it. Off with you to King's Ferry, Peekskill, and White Plains! Off with you both! Smith has mounts for both of you; and you'll be in the city in twelve hours. All the words have been said: the rest is action.

André. [*Shaking hands with* Arnold.] Till we meet again.

Arnold. [*With a gesture.*] There in the fort!
    Sir Henry on his horse,
And André like a Genius at his side,
Guiding the host! That flag shall fall
When next we meet: up run the British colors!
England forever! Heart, take heart, my lad!
We cannot fail. The rest is counting gains.

André. I think this exploit shall make England glad
When I'm in the grave.

Arnold. Odso! Our names shall chronicle the hills,
And school-boys learn us. Go in haste, good André!
Keep your mouth shut. Let Smith do all the talking.
These papers make you seem some Britisher,
An agent or a spy. You will be safe.
In every war are trusted underlings
Who pass from camp to camp like contraband;

Always suspected and yet always safe.

André. I like not such protection. Must I creep
  Beneath so mean a shelter,—seem a spy?
  I would to Heaven my purposes were known
  To every noble nature in the earth!

  Arnold. Off! And the nearest way!

  [Smith *changes* André's *coat.*]

  Success is virtue; and we mean to win.

  [*Exit* André _and _Smith.]

[*Aside.*] If we should fail, good youth, for history's eye,
  They'd write us up,—the traitor and the spy.
  Would God some power to telescope the hours
  Were lent me now! With André in New York
  I am revenged, rich, powerful, respected, everything
  My enemies begrudge. It cannot fail.
  O for a battle now to dry this sweat
  Of simple waiting! Sure, he cannot miss!
  My passes run the river up and down;
  And every day some messenger of mine
  Reaches New York; then why not he?
  If they should take him? But they *will* not take him.
  All these long months of waiting,—
  And not a soul to speak to; I could roar,—
  Sound it against the mountains,—that these peaks
  Should bandy my intentions back and forth;
  Or tell it to the talking cataracts
  To ease my need of speech. An hour's patience,
  Which seems as long as the preceding year,
  And I shall know. [*He sits down and
falls into a contemplation; then into a doze. As he falls asleep,
enter quietly* Treason.]

Arnold. [*Speaking as if out of his sleep.*]
    Leave me alone. Thou thing of little might!
  Thou painted bogey! I am conscience-proof,

26

And care no more what names I may be called.
If thou cans't make this hour glide more swift,
With idle chat of owls and haunted men,
I'll take thee for a gossip. Sit you there
And hide the hour-glass. There was a time
In early boyhood, when a thing like thee
Seemed horrible, but now my mouth is dry
With other terror. Thou art a cap and bells:
Play me a ditty on a tambourine.
[*Starting up.*] Who goes there?
[*Rushes to* Smith, *who enters.*]
Tell me that he is safe!

Joshua Smith. Within the lines, —
  Almost within the lines, — I left the youth.
  He's safe in British hands; and by his time,
  Is telling his adventures to Sir Henry.

Arnold. Ha, ha, ha, ha, ha! Is it not a joke, Joshua?
  Ha, ha, ha!
  This is a joke that shall run crackling through
  America, like Samson's burning foxes.
  Ha, ha, ha! — André is in New York!
  A spasm of joy; and yet it pains my leg.
  Your hand, my friend. The laughter comes again —
  Ha, ha, ha! Now let them vote! Brigadier Generals
  May rain on this accursed land of pain
  As fast as Congress spawns them! Now, ye rats!
  Who shall squirm last, I ask ye?
  [*To* Smith.] Safe, you say?
  You saw him with the British?

Smith. Not quite so;
  But at their outposts.

Arnold. It will take a day
  Before I can believe it. I am drunk
  With the intoxication of revenge,
  Sweeter than wine. A day of jubilee

Shall follow all our torments, Joshua Smith.
Out on ye, pack of curs! I have ye now,
Where ye'll not yelp so freely. — Ha, ha, ha —
Ha, ha, ha, ha! — And God I thank thee, too.
Justice is in the world.
Help me to the fortress. Mercy, how it pains!
Justice! Revenge! And, Joshua, — what a joke!

[*Exeunt* Arnold *and* Smith.]

Father Hudson. My heart is moved with sorrow: the sins of men enter into me and I am constrained. Why was this man chosen for suffering; and what balm is there for his seed?

Both Choruses. Fear God and seek not thine own advantage. Pluck not the grape thyself; for who knows whether it be intended for thee?

I will weep freely and lift up my voice for the sorrows of men. There is none that shall comfort me.

Come, Father, let us weep together and add our tears to thy streams; for so only can the medicine of this grief flow down to the children of men.

INTERMEZZO

Father Hudson. Is it finished?

Leader of Men. No; it is begun.

Father Hudson. His pain enters into me. I must endure these things. Woe is me that ever I was born of the brooks or received by the meadows! The pains of new birth get hold on me, and I see that life is sorrow. Why could ye not let me alone, ye pangs of knowledge; or go by on the other side, ye piercings of understanding? Must I be bound up forever with sin, and feel the hand of unevenness on my loins?

Both Choruses. So it is with all creatures of a deep spirit. They are caught with the net; they are frozen in the ice of God; they are very helpless, and cry for relief day and night.

Accept thy pains, for they are good. Reason not against fate but lay down thy will in earnest.

Father Hudson. Will the man come again?

Leader of Men. Once more shalt thou see him, and remember him forever. Lo, now he comes as the wounded lion, as the tiger bereft of his prey and wounded by the hunter. [*Enter* Arnold, *a pistol in one hand, a letter clutched in the other. During this speech he crosses the stage.*] His plot has failed and his iniquity is as a broken toy. Wrecked is all his life. He flees like a robber from his own land. Hills look your last upon Benedict! Ye Highlands, filled with clouds, and ye little streams that jet along the crags, this is your general. Will he remember you in his dreams, think you, or find himself back among you in his reveries? In his lone island, in his long years of silence, ye will return to him. Bid him adieu without bitterness, thou rocky castle! For his punishment shall be within himself day by day. [*Exit* Arnold.] Behold, [*Shades his eyes with his hand as if observing* Arnold] he is on the shore; his barge of eight oars obeys the signal; he stands in the prow; the rowers smite the water. With fury they row, for he commands them; with fury and terrible ire they row, for they fear the man. He has drawn a white handkerchief from his breast, though his pistol never leaves his hand. The prow of the British sloop of war looms above his barge. They see his signal. They are letting down the gangway. They are taking him up into the British vessel.

Chorus of Men. So down the torrent of infamy,
  So into the bosom of Hell,
  O *Vulture*, thou bearest him!

Chorus of Women. Naught brings he in hand to his captors;
  Naught but the coin of his soul;
  Empty-handed goeth he.

Chorus of Men. The great cheater here is cheated;
  The great traitor here betrayed:
  Where is his bargain?

Chorus of Women. Bare life he saves by the purchase,
  Merely the breath of life;
  Merely the fountain of pain.

Chorus of Men. Yea, out of the lips of aversion,
  Yea, out of the hand of contempt,
  He receiveth his price.

Chorus of Women. Pride is the hero's undoing,
  Pride is the sin of the great.
  Lo, he licketh the crumbs!

Both Choruses. So down the torrent of infamy,
  So into the bosom of Hell;
  O *Vulture*, thou bearest him!

  Father Hudson. Is all treason punished like this among men?

  Leader of Men. Father, thou askest things no man can answer.

  Father Hudson. If these things could be known, what man would follow his own desires? Fear overtaketh me in thinking of them. I thank the gods that my channel is laid, I cannot change it. The man seems to me like one who should place a lake on a hilltop and cry to it, Stay there! He hath wrestled against thunder. He would lift the rocks with his back; and he lies crushed beneath them. Can he not repent? Shall he never find out that fire is hot? Must he die still unapprised of his own foolishness?

Leader of Men. The future is a hard thing to know.

Father Hudson. Are there not charms that open mountain sides,
  And show what shall come forth?

Leader of Men. All things to come
  Are come already, — save the power to see them.

Father Hudson. Would I might know the ending of that man,
  Whose fate and story clinging to my name
  Do make me human!

Leader of Men. Human was his end,
  And very moving. Wouldst thou wait awhile,
  Or see the story now?

  Father Hudson. Now, now, my son!

Invocation. [*Sung in contralto voice, as before, by the* Leader of Women.] Storm-shadowed, precipitous valley, And ye threatening towers of stone that hold back the mountains, Letting the dark stream pass; Storm King, and Donderberg, homes of reverberant thunder; Thou steep theatre, where his story trod its stage, And where the circling thought of it returns With ever profounder, ever accumulating echoes, Calling to Humanity, compelling attention, provoking the unexpected tear,— Open yet once again your treasured legend; Out of the encrusted box, the precious parchment, Out of the vestment-chambers, the hallowed rags.

[*As the verse now changes its form, the music also slightly changes character.*]

Lo, now, our holiday calls on the past for its lessons,
  Lo, while the flame of the frost-bite fingers the dale,

Lo, in the lambent blaze of autumnal quiescence,
  Flows Father Hudson, at peace, through his populous vale.

Fruit trees garland his margins, — vines, and the brazen
  Hillocks of billowy rye o'er the undulous deep
Stretch to the Berkshires, proclaiming the conquering season;
  Dash on the Catskills, repulsed by the envious steep.

Woe, royal river! In grief I gaze on thy harvest,
  Anxious to me my thought as thy riches unroll.
Mortal, beware lest in riotous plenty thou starvest!
  Give me the fruits of the spirit, the songs of the soul.

Father Hudson. A sweet voice but sad, — trembling sad.

Leader of Men. Hush, it invokes the craggy wilderness,
  And seeks an entrance for its piercing cry.

Leader of Women. [*Sings. The music again changing with the metre.*]
  Give up the scene, give up, ye sordid rocks,
  The last of Arnold in his English home,
  Which in your bosom lives for evermore,
  A deathless picture; England cast it out
  Not being English, and it shivered on,
  Coiling about the world, till it was caught
  And locked into your rocky fastnesses
  Where it lives ever; and your mountain ribs
  Ache with the imposition.

ACT II

[_The centre of the stage slowly opens, disclosing a sitting-room.
A writing-table covered with letters. Somewhere in the foreground
a sofa or low couch: An engraved portrait of George III. *Arnold* is
sitting at the table, but his arm-chair is turned away. He is in a pro-
found reverie, gazing at the floor. He is dressed in the uniform of a
British officer. His hair is gray and his face worn. At the back of the
stage at one side of the door, sits *Treason*, somewhat in the attitude
of a sheriff's officer keeping guard._]

Treason. [*To* Arnold.]
  What are you muttering, comrade? Go to sleep!
  And yet sleep not too sound; there's work ahead!
  With all the world against us. What of that?
  We ne'er were beaten yet. Get money first:
  A fortune in your fist. With honest luck,
  Your hand against the world! But money first.
  [*Aside.*] He breaks apace, and I await each day
  The knock of Death —
  [*Knocking.*] No, no, not yet, Sir Death!
  There's life in him and, mayhap, years of grief.
  Leave me to tousle him. He's strong as hemp
  And bears his ragging well.
  [*More knocking.*] Not yet, not yet!

[*Enter* Death.]

Treason. You are unjust to come before the time.

Death. The moment and myself are on the stroke.

Treason. Thou deemest that this man is soon to die?

Death. Death is already in him.

Treason. Yea, his body. — His mind is brighter than it was before.

Death. My shadow lights his mind; but it is Death.

Treason. How hast thou entered him without a struggle?

Death. The struggle was thy work.

Treason. Give me some moments.

Death. [*Pointing to the door with great dignity.*] The man is mine.
Hence! Silence! Obey!

[*Exit* Treason. Death_ takes *Treason's* place by the door._]

Arnold. [*Waking.*] They deny me the opportunity of honorable death.
  This is the twentieth year of sodden waiting.
  Fighting by land and sea and soldier's work,
  As hot as heart could wish, — boy generals, —
  Wars on all hands, in Holland, France, and Spain,
  With military honors falling thick; —
  And I, a Tantalus set in a lake of thirst,
  Up to my neck in battles all about,
  Without the power to reach them!

[*Enter* Mrs. Arnold. *She has a youthful face, and her hair is prematu-
rely white. She passes by* Death _without seeing him. A gesture of
surprise and pity as she sees* Arnold. *She kisses him on his forehead,
and sits down next him on a lower chair._*]

Mrs. Arnold. Surely, my husband you have not been forth!
  After the sullen fever you have had
  'Twas most unwise. —
  [*Pause.*]
  You have been grieved, and wear the ashen look.

Arnold. Age, and the chafing of a few stern thoughts.

Mrs. Arnold. Have I not earned the right to know them?

Arnold. Indeed, thou hast! An angel from the sky
  Accepting the bad bargain of a man,
  Could not have found a worse. You took me up
  A battered piece of ordnance, broken in spirit,
  Accursed to myself and to my kind;
  And underneath me thou hast held an arm
  Sustaining as the seraph's upward look

34

Askance against Apollyon.

Mrs. Arnold. Benedict!
  You shall not talk so. —

Arnold. Next, your mother's heart
  Became the mother to my three grown boys,
  Giving them such devotion and such love
  As rarely flows from out a mother's hope
  To her own children.

Mrs. Arnold. Benedict, your words
  Cut me like knives. Why, why this catalogue?

    Arnold. Something compels me. —

Mrs. Arnold. Where have you been?
  Has some insulting taunt
  Cast by a coward in a public place
  Where you could not resent it, stung your patience?
  These are the pebbles small men throw at great.

Arnold. No. 'Tis the season for my wounds to ache;
  And with them aches the rest. —

    Mrs. Arnold. Where have you been?

    Arnold. Three hours in his Lordship's ante-room.

    Mrs. Arnold. The War Office? And what has been decided?

Arnold. I could not see his Lordship. Three hours late.
  They sent me word his Lordship was not in.
  It is the iteration wears me down.
  Year after year, — year after leaden year, —
  Kicking my heels in England's ante-rooms,
  Where proud men pass me by: and now and then
  I catch a glimpse of some American, —
  A former pal, a former enemy; —
  It is the same, both pal and enemy

Give me a fit of trembling. 'Twas not so;
Yet as the years decline our nerves grow sick:
I dread it more and more.

Mrs. Arnold. O Benedict,
  This is the mood that kills us. Have we not
  A thousand times resolved it, made all plain?
  You in your right of conscience chose a course
  Beside your King, recanting many errors,
  And following the only light you knew.
  The king himself accepted your return
  And raised you with his hand.

  Arnold. [*Very quietly.*] I was a traitor.

  Mrs. Arnold. [*With great vehemence.*] No, no, no! You were the nob-
lest hero of them all!

  Arnold. And now they do not trust me.

  Mrs. Arnold. Is there a soldier in the British Isles That has a list of
battles like your own?

  Arnold. It may be not.

Mrs. Arnold. Then make allowances for jealousy.
  To Englishmen, their battles are a sport,
  With every post of danger dearly prized,
  Like the crack stations in the shooting field,—
  Never enough for all. They bribe and jockey,—
  Knife their own brothers to get near the spoil.
  And would they not repel a foreigner,—
  One they had cause to envy? Englishmen
  Are very unforgiving of defeat.
  It is your glory, the impediment:
  So gluttonous are soldiers of reward—
  So sporting-keen are Englishmen for fame.

  Arnold. It may be so.

Mrs. Arnold. Your temperament is of colossal mould, And sees too simply.

Arnold. I was a traitor.

Mrs. Arnold. Are you a man to take the common talk,
  And be its dupe? How often have we spoke
  Of the returning wars that shall restore
  The lustred fame and power that is your due?
  Belated are they; yet to reason's eye
  Certain to come. God keeps such eminence
  As in your soul exists, to show mankind
  The height of heroes.

  Arnold. Error: it is gone out.

Mrs. Arnold. Never such light goes out! No smoke of the world—
  Sin, error, evil, anguish, touch it not.
  It burns forever with ethereal force
  Beyond pollution. I can see your soul;
  And never has its aspect been more bright
  Than on this morn.

  Arnold. You are not used to talk to me like this.

  Mrs. Arnold. Nor you to tell me that you are a traitor.

  Arnold. Perhaps some change is coming over us.

  Mrs. Arnold. It may be freedom from the load of thought.

  Arnold. It may be death.

  [*She kneels by him in silent anguish.*]

  Both Choruses. Surely truth is not born except through pain; and the long delay increaseth it.

  It is a happiness for a young man to see his error. But for an old, only death remains. He hath no strength for new things. Let him die in his old ways, yea, though they be evil.

Very sad is repentance when it is too late; when the blight has fallen, and no fruit cometh thereafter. Very sad is the grief of an old man. I cannot lay hold of it. There is no comfort to be given him, for he knoweth the world.

Father Hudson. What causes the man to see these things now?

Leader of Men. What causes thy waters to pour down in March, or the leaf upon your banks to sprout in April? It is because the season fulfils itself; and what is to be, cometh forth, and no one may stop it.

Both Choruses. Now may I say that no man is made of iron, or lives beyond the stroke of reproach.

The arrows strike him when he shows it not. The scornful glance of a friend reaches his quick. He suffers very much.

In his last days he betrayeth the havoc. In his fall his wounds are laid bare. The secret of his heart becomes an open book, and a child may read it.

Arnold. I would not speak; but the sea-bottom of me
  Is being raked to the surface. Hold you still;
  You are the daughter of good Tory folk,
  And common talk on King and loyalty
  Had in your ears a meaning and a place
  Quite strange to mine. For my Rhode Island stock,
  Grown far afield, and long acclimated,
  Had dropped all meanings for the name of King,
  Of Church, of mother country. Such appeals
  Were like a tinsel fringe of superstition,
  Alien imposture. It was all a fraud.

[*He walks across the room, takes the portrait of George III and throws it, not savagely, but with deliberate contempt, into the corner, where it lies shattered. Mrs.* Arnold *remains on her knees and raises her hands in helpless supplication.*]

There lies the dog that bit me. Now desist:
It is not easy; yet it must come out.
A letter that I wrote to this same King,

Or to his secretary, George Germain, —
Imploring favors for my villainy —
If I appear unmanned, it's physical,
And needs no moment's thought — The letter's here,
[*Takes a letter from his pocket.*]
And through its hell of shame as through a gate
I see Elysian fields, peopled with comrades.

Mrs. Arnold. [*Aside.*] God have mercy upon us!

Arnold. I'll not read all, but phrases here and there.

[Arnold *reads from the letter with some difficulty and with pauses —
but very distinctly.*]

"… conscious of the rectitude of my intentions…. that I may be
restored to the favor of my most Gracious Sovereign — … cheerfully
cast myself at his feet imploring his Royal Grace and Protection….
the unalterable attachment to the Person, Family, and Interests of
my Sovereign, and to the Glory of his reign. — …"

[*He throws the letter quietly on the table. To* Mrs. Arnold.]

West Point I did deliberately betray:
I begged the post intending to betray it.
All was conceived before I married you.

Mrs. Arnold. [*As before.*] God have mercy upon us!

Arnold. They must pet me then,
  To show that loyal treason reaps reward.
  'Twas policy, not liking for my face,
  That made King George so sweet.
  What in this world of savage Englishmen,
  Strange monsters that they are, have you and I
  Found of a country? Friends, good hearts and true;
  But alien as the mountains of the moon,
  More unrelated than the Polander,
  Are Englishmen to us. They are a race,
  A selfish, brawling family of hounds,
  Holding a secret contract on each fang,

'For us,' 'for us,' 'for us.' They'll fawn about;
But when the prey's divided; — Keep away!
I have some beef about me and bear up
Against an insolence as basely set
As mine own infamy; yet I have been
Edged to the outer cliff. I have been weak,
And played too much the lackey. What am I
In this waste, empty, cruel, land of England,
Save an old castaway, — a buccaneer, —
The hull of derelict Ambition, —
Without a mast or spar, the rudder gone,
A danger to mankind!

[*He sits down upon the couch.* Mrs. Arnold *throws herself on his knees and sobs convulsively.*]

Both Choruses. Who shall praise a woman, save He that made her, save God that understandeth all things?

I will sing a song of woman, and magnify the wife of a man's soul. His goodness she has discerned when no man else can find it: his crimes are known to her, yet is he not in them: she seeketh his soul among many.

She divineth salvation out of hell; and bringeth water from the desert. Who shall praise a woman save He that made her; save God who understandeth all things?

Father Hudson. Sorrow is erecting a tomb for this man in my heart. Whence comes the peculiar pang, my children? Whence comes this pity that will not be denied, but bedews your faces?

Leader of Men. From the greatness of the man, comes it Father; and from his ignorance of himself.

Father Hudson. Is it true that he was a hero?

Leader of Men. Such a hero as antiquity can show, towering, magnificent, made of cloud and thunder, made of lightning and glory, a god among fighting men, a Hector or Mars appearing from the bosom of the sky on the day of battle, bringing victory.

No one had seen his like before; nor since him has one like him come. To his country he gave the column of his strength. In her need he sustained her. He planted her high. His name became bulwark: many times gave he his strength. Yea, his life also grudged he not.

Father Hudson. Would he had died in his glory, would he had been struck down and died long ago! So had he been spared this humiliation. On my shores he belongs: the memory of his infamy and of his fame covers me: Saratoga knew him, and West Point acknowledges him. No tomb shall he have; yet shall the hills remember him. His glory is eaten up in shame; and yet shall mercy say her word. See, he begins again. What new anguish will he reveal?

Arnold. [*He has now recovered his composure.*]
  Where are the boys? If death be soon to come
  I'd gladly see them. Is it not most strange
  That one possessing nothing to bequeath
  Of all those things men covet for their sons,
  Should have so many? For what rank or name,
  Honor or fatherland, or worldly goods,
  All that men sweat for, — have I here to leave?
  Country I've none. My land was over there
  Where my first honors sprouted. And my boys
  Are foreigners, — young Englishmen — brought up
  Upon King George's bounty. When he bought
  My loyalty he took my children, too.
  Ben, he is dead, my eldest, — he was killed
  In the West Indies, fighting for the King.
  Sir Grenville Temple brought me back his sword.
  (God bless him for it!) Send and fetch down Ben's sword.

  [Mrs. Arnold *rings. Enter servant. She speaks to servant in dumbshow. Exit servant.*]

  Richard and Henry, your two foster sons,
  Settled in Canada on royal grants.
  And our four sons, — your Edward, Robert, George
  And little William, — are all pensioners,

Assisted servants of the English crown.
Where are they? I must see them. It is strange
That I, remembering them, can yet not think
Quite plainly where they are.

Mrs. Arnold. My dearest Lord
There's fever in your cheek. The day's distress
Has worked some downfall to your shattered brain,
You're very sick. —

Arnold. The boys, I asked about —
Are they away, or here?

Mrs. Arnold. The elder three
At school and college, and our little Will
Just home from school.

Arnold. I pray you let him come;
My blessings on them all must fall through him;
Nor will they wait: the passage of an hour
May find me gone. —Stay; there is yet one son.

Mrs. Arnold. No, Benedict, you have described them all.

Arnold. Ay, but there is one, born in Canada,
My natural son, whose mother is no more;
And yet my son, —and brother to the rest,
And ever at my cost I've brought him up.
I cannot leave him out. He is of age
And elder than your boys.

Mrs. Arnold. A son of yours —

Arnold. A natural son of mine, whose bringing up
Is at my charge. I cannot cut him off.
Though of my name I scanted him the curse,
I ever sent him help.

[*Gives her a paper.*]

42

Mrs. Arnold. You have done right
  To count him in; and I accept him,
  And will provide a portion like the rest
  Though at my children's cost.

Arnold. Send William here:
  The time grows short.

  [*Enter servant bringing the sword which* Mrs. Arnold *takes and gives to* Arnold.]

  Mrs. Arnold. [*To servant.*] Send Master William here.

  [*Exit servant. Enter* William Arnold, *a boy of eight.*]

Arnold. William, you are a soldier: —
  This old sword
  Was once your brother Ben's, — my eldest boy.
  He scrved his God, his Country, and his King,
  And found a soldier's death. It is a record
  We may be proud of in the family.
  You and your brothers, Edward, George, and Robert,
  Are dedicated soldiers to the King.
  England, to all of you, is generous
  To overflowing: See ye pay her back
  In overflowing measure with your lives.
  You are a soldier, Sir, and understand
  The duties of a soldier; when you grow
  A little older you will read, perhaps,
  Something about your father; for his name
  Is written on a page of history;
  You cannot miss it. When you find it there,
  Remember only all the soldier part;
  The soldier part he leaves you: all the rest
  Was something suffered, that was meant for him
  But not for you. There, go my boy; good-bye.
  You must to all your brothers tell this news,
  And say I blessed them. They will understand,
  Each in his measure, on the appointed day,
  My message to them. See you bear it safe.

It is a charge of honor and becomes you.

[Arnold *kisses the little boy, and gives him the sword with which he walks toward the door. The child feels that something very serious is happening, although he does not entirely understand it. When near the door he turns, runs back and embraces the old man again; and then exit.*]

Both Choruses. Now will I say that children add to life a glory not belonging to it; and a pang beyond the pain of this world.

In them is pain; in their birth, danger; and in their tender years, a care; thereafter, sorrow or joy, too keen, too keen, too poignant, too sharp, — cutting the heart in twain.

Happy are they who know it not. Happy are the childless; for the great sufferings are kept from them. Blessed are they: I will praise and envy them always.

Arnold. Now is my burden lightened.
  One adieu, —
  The worst, remains; and then, — I know not what, — some relaxation
  Or sweetness of the grave.
  [*To* Mrs. Arnold.] Good-bye, great soul;
  I leave thee sorrows, many-pointed cares,
  The stress of growing sons and straightening means;
  Yet one great blackness passes from your life,
  Unshadowing you all. I see ye stand
  Safe in the port, — as on a margent shore
  Clustered in sunlight, — while my bark moves on.
  I am not of ye; I am far away
  And long ago; one of those Argonauts
  That in the western seas, with sturdy oar,
  Urging their venturesome and sacred bark,
  Steered a new course, — a band, a brotherhood, —
  And, though a Judas, I was one of them.
  Get me my uniform. I wore it last
  On that last day on which my sun went down.

And I, descending now to seek the sun,
  Must put it on.

Mrs. Arnold. Dear Benedict, your uniform?
  You have it on.

Arnold. No, no! not this, not this!
  Ring; call a servant!

Mrs. Arnold. [*Rings. To servant.*]
  Whate'er he asks for, get it quickly for him,
  But make no questions.

  [Arnold *speaks to servant in dumb-show. Exit servant.*]

Arnold. The very coat I did the treason in,
  By accident preserved, and then, — and then —
  I could not cast it off: it clung to me —
  Waiting this day. It lay there like a dog,
  Patient against a master's drunkenness,
  Watching his face.

  [*Enter servant with the coat of the American uniform, and the sword-
knots.*]

Thou one unbroken link with all the men
I walked with on the mountain heights of youth,
When glory shone, and trumpets heralded,
And drums were rolling! We were patriots then,
Warren, and Putnam, Lincoln, Knox, and Schuyler,
Morgan, and Stark, Montgomery, Sullivan —
And scores of faces burnished by the winds,
That shone with glory —

  [*He takes off the coat of his British uniform, the servant assisting, and
puts on the coat of his old American uniform.*]

          Never weep, dear wife.
  I seek the truth you teach me. It is thus

Your thoughts do guide me;—and I must go back
To where I lost the way.
[*Showing sword-knots.*] That ornament
Washington gave me,—with such words of praise
As must preserve it till the judgment day
Against corruption. Should I meet that man,
Will his reluctant and offended shade
Pass sadly on? Or will he greet me there,—
There, but not here. There, there, but never here!
On toward that shadowy spot I blindly go,
Claiming the past.

[*He lies down on the couch, and* Mrs. Arnold *kneels by his side. Exit* Death.]

Both Choruses. Surely the past must be allowed to all men; and not to him alone. What good there was in us cannot be lost.

God forgets not the virtue of those who have failed; and why should man seek to judge them? Verily all courage is immortal: the man himself cannot kill it.

Lo, what great things are done through even bad men; and this man had in him much goodness.

[*A pause. Distant military music. Four young boys dressed in white, and bearing tall spears with little banners attached to the tips, enter and stand each at one corner of the couch. The arrangement suggests a medieval church tomb, of which* Mrs. Arnold's *kneeling figure forms a part.*]

Both Choruses. Not on the shores of America—
Not on our shuddering strand,
Can Arnold's tomb be laid.

Nor in his land of illusions—
Britain's contemptuous Isle,
Can stone be added to stone.

Yet in a corner of Memory,
Hallowed by terrible pain,
  Stand the stones of his grave.

There, his trophies of victory,
Piled in marshal array,
  Gorgeous, perennial —

Spoils, heroic, tumultuous,
Emblems, worthy remembrance —
  Marking a hero's grave.

[*While this is being sung there enters a procession of youths dressed in white, each carrying a gigantic wreath, inscribed with one of* Arnold's *victories: — The Maine Wilderness, Quebec, Valcour's Island, St. John's, Ridgefield, Bemis Heights, Saratoga, etc. They circle the group, and pile the wreaths about the couch, then stand about in symmetry.*]

Father Hudson. Enough, my children, I understand. Leave me awhile. Let there be no loud praises. Go silently.

[*A dead march is played.* Father Hudson *resumes the plastic, immobile, and almost invisible attitude which he occupied at the opening of the play. The* Choruses *file silently out, one on each side of the orchestra.*]

THE END

Books by John Jay Chapman

EMERSON AND OTHER ESSAYS

CAUSES AND CONSEQUENCES

PRACTICAL AGITATION

FOUR PLAYS FOR CHILDREN

THE MAID'S FORGIVENESS, a play

A SAUSAGE FROM BOLOGNA, a play

LEARNING AND OTHER ESSAYS

THE TREASON AND DEATH OF BENEDICT ARNOLD, a play for a Greek theatre

Moffat, Yard & Co.,

NEW YORK